Existence of Unnatural

A collection of short stories

[*Some are based on true incidents*]

AF656845

By

PRITAM MUKHERJEE

This novel is entirely a work of fiction. The names, characters, organizations and incidents portrayed in it are the work of the author's imagination. Any resemblance to actual persons, living or dead, events or localities, is entirely coincidental.

The views expressed in this book are entirely those of the author. The printer/publisher, and distributors of this book are not in any way responsible for the views expressed by the author in this book. All disputes are subject to arbitration; legal actions if any are subject to the jurisdictions of courts of Kolkata, India.

ISBN: 978-93-84333-88-1

Edited by:
Victor Mukherjee & Pritam Mukherjee

Dedicated

To my Family, Friends &

Beloved Readers

PREFACE & ACKNOWLEDGENTS

Unnatural things happen in many persons' lives. Some people regard them to be unnatural and believe them while others throw it out of their mind and make certain assumptions. Some people believe in spirits and Gods while others do not but when a topic of an unnatural occurrence comes up, everyone gets interested. The non-believers also listen to the topic carefully and then go onto create a logic behind everything.

However this is my first book and I have come up with some stories that I have heard to be true and some stories with my own imagination. Personally, I also did not believe in ghosts or spirits but after brainstorming a lot I came up with a scientific explanation about life which may or may not be true. The end chapter comprises of my scientific explanations of life. This book is however not intended to promote any beliefs in unnatural occurrences but just to read and enjoy as a story book.

I am grateful to my family a lot who has always supported me in whatever I did and without their motivation I would not have started writing this book. I am also grateful to my office colleagues who have given me motivation and support to write this book. I also thank all who have made it possible to publish my book.

Hope everyone enjoys the book.......Best wishes for all!

CONTENTS

Haunted House at Ashoknagar

[Based on a story which is claimed to be true]

It was during the seventies. The Naxalbari revolutionary movement was going on in West Bengal at that time. My father had just entered in his college and he also got involved in that movement. He had many friends at Ashoknagar, a place in West Bengal and they invited him on Kali Puja at their place. Two of his friends were very close to him named Chhotka and Borka. My father was from Kolkata and hence the people over there called him Shohorer babu, meaning a person from city. He enjoyed a lot over there and defeated the villagers in swimming and climbing upon trees though they were experts in those activities.

At the end of the day, it was time to get things ready for the Puja. It was a moonless night as Kali Puja is done in a moonless night and it gets chillier at that time of the season. Winter gets around the corner in West Bengal at the time of Kali Puja. After all the things were arranged, everyone sat down to chat near the temple. One of the villagers said to my father, "You are a very brave person. You have defeated us all in the activities in which we are expert at but your bravery can only be proved if you spend one night at the haunted house in our locality." He quickly turned to Chhotka and said, "Didn't you tell him about the haunted house in our locality?" My father asked Chhotka, "Which house is he talking about?" He got very much interested. Borka then replied, "It is a house near the railway station. The house is really haunted and whoever had been to the house saw ghosts. Some of them had become mad forever and others were found in unconscious state, who went to spend a night in the house accepting challenges from others." My father then said to him, "What does really happen over there that people become mad or lose consciousness?" Chhotka then said, "It was a house of the Zamindars. There is a huge Naach Mahal in the house and people who became unconscious, said that the Naach Mahal became lively after half past one in the night. The dancers and musicians seemed to come to the Naach Mahal and perform." One of the villagers then said to my father, "Are you willing to spend the night in the haunted house? We will then accept that you are very brave." My father immediately agreed in the affirmative but Borka stopped him. He said, "It's not a matter of joke. Unnatural things really happened in that house and moreover; if something happens then who will take the responsibility?" My father then said that he would take his own responsibility and assured that nothing would happen to him but he would need a few things like a torch, a stick, a knife, a revolver or a pistol and some food to spend the night in the house. They all agreed and went to Somnathda for the purpose of getting those things.

Somnathda was a political person and he possessed a revolver. They narrated the whole thing to him that my father would spend the whole night in that haunted house at his own risk but wanted his revolver for the night. Somnathda initially refused to part with his revolver and warned my father to change his decision. My father was determined to stay in the house. Somnathda finally agreed and asked whether my father knew how to fire. My father answered him in the affirmative. Somnathda wanted him to fire a blank fire handing him over his revolver. He did so and Somnathda was quick to understand my father's political background. He handed him over his revolver and also gave six more bullets in case he needed more. Somnathda also gave his twelve-battery torch to him. He also instructed others to stay nearby the house as it was a very infamous house in the locality.

They all went towards the house. Others stopped about quite a distance from the house. It was a huge area surrounded by boundary walls. In the middle was the house standing in a dilapidated condition. The area used to have a garden but then it was more or less like a jungle as there was no maintenance. There was a huge iron gate. My father pushed the gate with all his might but could not open it. It was totally jammed due to rust. Then he kicked the gate with tremendous power and then the gate somewhat loosened up a bit. Again he pushed with all his power and the gate slowly opened up enough for him to squeeze in. Huge trees and bushes covered up the entire area. It was even darker as it was a moonless night. He lit the torch and tapped the stick on the ground, checking all around and slowly approached towards the house because there could be snakes. He then came in front of the main door. The main door was jammed too and hence he used his force again to open the main door of the house. Just after entering the house he found a room on the right hand side. He thought whether to take shelter in that room but then decided to check the house first. The twelve-battery torch provided enough light to see everything. The house was completely in a dilapidated condition and weeds were growing everywhere. Roots of weeds were also hanging from the ceilings. There was a huge staircase going upstairs. My father then went up and saw a huge veranda. He walked through the veranda and found the Naach Mahal. He opened the door and found no one. He saw that the Naach Mahal had stairs going upstairs and had balconies from where the audience used to watch the performances. My father went up to check if anyone was there or not hiding to frighten him. He found no one and went out of the Naach Mahal closing the door partly. Beside the Naach Mahal was another room which even had a bed but without any mattress. He decided to stay in that room and cleaned the bed to relax on it. He had taken a lot of fruits along with him and hence started to cut them with his knife to have them for dinner. He was relishing on the nice fruits when he saw that it was half past one on his wrist watch. According to the stories, it was time and so he became alert.

Suddenly a sound of ankle bells was heard by him. It sounded as if someone was walking down the veranda and approaching towards the Naach Mahal. He started to feel tensed but prepared himself mentally. He took out the revolver and crept towards the door of his room as silently as possible. He opened the door a bit to see who it was. What he saw was a hazy and shadowy figure of a dancing girl approaching towards the Naach Mahal. She entered the Naach Mahal and soon after another dancing girl followed. She was also coming down by the veranda with ankle bells bound on her feet and entered the Naach Mahal. Like that six girls entered the Naach Mahal. Then the sound of harmonium, sitar, tabla and dancing of the girls started to come from the Naach Mahal. My father got out of the room and approached towards the Naach Mahal to check what was really going on. He found that the door of the Naach Mahal was completely closed which he had left partly opened. He pushed the door to open it slowly as he did not want to make any noise distracting them. He was amazed to see the chandelier glowing though not lit and it filled the Naach Mahal with enough light. The hazy and shadowy figures of the girls were dancing to the music being played by the hazy and shadowy figures of the musicians. He rushed towards the centre shouting, "Who are you all?" Everyone vanished in a split of a second and a huge laughter of many men and women reverberated in the entire Naach Mahal. The Naach Mahal had an iron stairs leading to the backyard and he immediately rushed towards the stairs. He found no one though he decided to check the backyard if anyone was there or not.

He started to go down by the stairs. Climber plants clutched the stairs all over making it difficult for him to go down but slowly he managed somehow. He checked everywhere in the backyard with the torch but could not see anyone. He moved forward a bit to check if someone was hiding. After walking some distance he saw a hut and the light of the torch flashed in one's face. The person screamed in fear, "Ghost, ghost". My father replied that he was a human being and not a ghost. The person then asked him what he was doing there in the middle of the night. He said that he had come to spend a night in that haunted house. The person immediately warned him to go back and not be foolish to spend the night there but he refused to hear his words and went back to the house again. It was a difficult task to climb that iron stairs again and so he decided to get into the house through the main door.

He entered the house again and went up the staircase. Suddenly there was a hazy and shadowy figure coming down by the staircase. He immediately stretched out his hand to stop him. It seemed that a strong wind pushed his hand with a great jerk and he lost his balance. The shadowy figure vanished in no time and a huge laughter roared in the entire house. The laughter echoed again and again in the empty misty dilapidated house. My father could not believe what he was experiencing. He again went up and stopped at the veranda. From the veranda, he checked every nook and corner of the ground floor again with the torch light. There was none. He walked up to the Naach Mahal again. No one was there even. The chandelier was also not glowing. He could not understand what he saw or felt was true or not and then went back to the room in which he was taking shelter for the night. He found almost all the fruits that he cut were gone. He thought that it might have been eaten up by the rats in the house. He again took out some of the fruits and started to cut and have them.

After about fifteen minutes or so, the music started again. The sound of dancing was again coming from the Naach Mahal. My father again went out of his room and went towards the Naach Mahal. He opened the door and saw the same scene. The shadowy figures of musicians and dancers were performing in the middle and the chandelier was glowing. He did not shout that time. He watched on for about five minutes looking at every corner of the Naach Mahal to check whether the visionaries were made by any audio-visual aid or not. Finding nothing, he decided to fire at the chandelier. He pulled the trigger and the chandelier fell down breaking into pieces. The images all vanished following a huge laughter of many men and women that reverberated in the entire house that time. Suddenly a pin drop silence followed in the entire house. He again went back to his room but his mind was clouded by the experiences he had gathered. After that nothing happened. It was ten past four in the morning and he was feeling sleepy. He then decided to leave the premises as the night was already over.

He then left the premises of the house. He found everyone sitting at quite a distance from the house. Somnathda was also sitting and waiting for his arrival. On his arrival, Somnathda said to him, "Are you alright?" He replied that he was fine and said that he had to fire a bullet. Borka asked him, "What happened? What did you see?" He then narrated to them everything that had happened in the night. He still ponders even today what he experienced on that night was in real or was that man-made to frighten people because after he shot at the chandelier, nothing happened thereafter. Since then everyone respected my father at Ashoknagar and agreed that he was indeed a brave person.

Haunted Murder

[Based on a story which is claimed to be true]

After a long while, all of our friends finally got some holidays to enjoy from the humdrum life. We chose a resort in the islands of Lakshadweep. Being with friends after a long time was one of the most satisfying moments of my life. The resort was booked by Rahul, one of our friends and he was our main guide as we knew nothing about the islands. Only he knew about the place as he had been to the place quite often and it was his favourite holiday destination. It was he who insisted upon us all to go to the Lakshadweep islands. We had all agreed to visit the Lakshadweep islands because a place not seen is always a good place to spend time during a holiday. We decided to go to the island by ship as we all had never travelled by a ship before. We all wanted to make that trip something special so that we could all remember that trip throughout our lives.

Rahul on the way was describing how beautiful the place is. The sand is white and the water of the sea surrounds the whole of the islands and is perfectly blue. On the other part of the island the colour of the sea is green which makes a unique blend of picturesque place. He was however sad because he could not book his favourite resort as it was previously booked by others.

The ship arrived at the port around three in the afternoon. The port was also beautiful. We set forth for our resort. The sea beach was splendid and as Rahul described, it was really a picturesque place. Had we not agreed to visit there we would have really missed to view such a lovely place. We arrived at the resort by dusk but the very first look of the resort gave me an eerie feeling. I did not like the look of the resort at all.

The resort was surrounded with long eucalyptus trees which was pretty weird as in an island there should be coconut trees mainly. Moreover on our way to the resort, we saw mostly coconut trees but there we found only eucalyptus trees. The walls of the resort were decorated with chopped off heads of hunted beasts which were well lively. It seemed as if the beasts were staring at us angrily and some had terrible sorrow in their eyes. That could be well felt and we all looked at each other because we were not feeling comfortable. However Rahul was not at all bothered by those feelings of us. He was very much overjoyed to be back at his favourite destination and to enjoy his holidays that time with us. The manager of the resort greeted us and showed us our rooms but one room which seemed to be the best room in the resort from outside was completely sealed. That made us very curious and wanted the manager to open the room. The manager denied to do so and warned us several times not to open the room. That increased our curiosity further and we forcibly opened the lock of the room.

That was really the best room of the resort. The view of the sea-shore from the balcony of the room was spectacular. The lights coming from the light-house and ships at distant were wonderful to watch for in the darkness over the sea. The sunshine in the morning could also be viewed from the balcony only which would be a great feeling with the morning tea. The room was also adorned with a nice arm-chair and we immediately all agreed to stay in that room. The manager pleaded and warned us not to stay in that room several times but when we asked the reason why we should not stay in the room, he kept mum and told that he could not give any specific reason. Thus we turned a deaf ear to his warnings.

The manager went back to his room and we enjoyed ourselves thoroughly. We sang, danced, played the guitar and cracked a lot of jokes laughing at each other, shared and revived the old joyful memories and sorrows of our old times. We gave the order of our dinner and dinner was available in no time. It was a nice dinner as well with rice, chicken and sausages. After dinner we sat down together chatting and having fun again. Rahul sat on the arm-chair and the rest of us were either on the floor or on the bed. He was telling that we must go out fishing on the next day as it was a great fun fishing in that place. He showed us that he had brought his fishing kit along with him and also bought a few extra for us also. Suddenly the lights went off and we all went mum. A cold breeze started to blow inside the room and we were all having a shivering feeling in us. However we started to look for our bags and searched for the candles that we had taken along with us. After five minutes of searching we got the candles and lit up two of them. Suddenly a sound started like someone was walking and coming close to our room. At first we thought of the manager but the sound was very odd. It was like a person walking with a wooden leg. There was no one with a wooden leg in the resort. The servants were already gone after serving us the dinner. They did not stay in the resort except for the manager who had a separate room just outside the compound of the resort. The sound of the footsteps stopped just in front of our door. We asked who it was but there was no reply. The door was locked from inside but the lock could be seen clearly opening on its own in the candlelight. Fear gripped us immediately and we started to scream but Rahul got stuck in the chair. The door slammed open but no one could be seen. We all tried to pull out Rahul but in vain. He was completely stuck. He was screaming on top of his voice and was crying out loud that someone was holding him back in the chair but we could not see anything of that sort. The sound of the footsteps slowly entered the room and Rahul could be seen getting strangled in the candle-light. We immediately rushed to the manager's room in fear.

When we came back, we found Rahul sitting on the chair lying dead. Police were informed and the body was sent for post-mortem. The manager then told us that that was the room of the resort's owner who had a wooden leg and had died in a car accident a month ago. That arm-chair was his favourite and liked no one to sit on it and that was why he was warning us not to stay in that room. The post-mortem report concluded that Rahul died due to heart-attack who was twenty-seven years old and had no heart-related problems. We all wanted to make that trip special. That trip really had been special and we can never forget in our lives but on a different note.

Dwarkanath Bose Lane, Cossipore

[Based on a story which is claimed to be true]

I was then six years old. At that time we were tenants and we resided at Burrabazar, a place in Kolkata. The house in Burrabazar was a damp one and I got attacked by double pneumonia and hence the doctor had advised my family to move to a better place. Therefore we decided to shift to a better place as tenants only and we came to that house at Dwarkanath Bose Lane, Cossipore. The address of that very place still haunts me even today. My maternal grand-mother used to stay along with us during those days and she only used to take care of me as my mother used to stay busy cooking food and doing all her house-hold activities throughout the day. When we came to that house my grand-mother said to my mother that she did not like the house very much. She did not feel nice about the place as she had an eerie feeling.

We were not the only tenants of the house. It also had two other families as tenants. Both the families came one month before our arrival as tenants. One family consisted of only husband and wife and the other family had some more people in the family. The family which consisted of only husband and wife were at war between each other always. The land-lady of the house dwelled in the topmost floor of the building and she was alone. She was an old lady around sixty three years of age which I remember. The structure of the house was very much like that of the old houses in Kolkata. The middle of the house had a huge open space. The lane outside the house could be well viewed from the stairs. My father used to stay busy all day long at his automobile repairing workshop and hence he hardly paid any heed to my grand-mother's words that the house was not good. However he assured that he was looking for a better house than that one as he did not like to stay with other tenants and not for the reason of my grand-mother's words. He said that he did not believe in those sorts of words.

The first day in the morning I had gone to the latrine and there I had a strange feeling. It seemed as if someone else was sitting beside me. I turned immediately but there was none. I got very scared but could not do much because I knew that no one would believe me that there was someone sitting beside me in the latrine as no one could be seen. However I came out quickly and told my grand-mother about the feeling but she only told me to be brave and assured me that there was no one as I had predicted.

Every day and night after, we could hear some very peculiar noises as if someone was whispering, talking, laughing or weeping. We never spoke much about those things amongst ourselves though we all felt those things regularly. We could only assure our minds that those were our hallucinations only and not happening in real.

Those things however continued but we did not know at that time what dangerous events were in store for us to experience. The days were coming closer to the ultimate day and peculiar happenings started to increase. The windows and doors opened upon themselves quite often. The sounds of weeping were becoming clearer but we only kept on thinking that those events were happening by sudden winds though we all knew deep in our hearts that it was not done by winds. One day while my mother was cooking in the kitchen, Haru uncle cut his leg very deeply. He was the husband of Protima aunty who were always at war between each other. Immediately the war between them resumed and Haru uncle was accusing Protima aunty that she was responsible for the cut. We ran to their room and found Haru uncle's leg bleeding profusely. He was claiming that she had kept the kitchen-knife on the floor carelessly and as a result his leg had got cut but she was completely on the denial. She could clearly remember that she had kept the knife in the kitchen. She was herself astonished how the knife could have come in the bed-room but Haru uncle got even more furious at that remark of his wife. He inquired whether the knife had got legs and walked into the room cutting his leg deeply. The war grew fiercely and both of them almost took to blows. They were however pacified by others in the house and the natural habit of uncle Haru followed. Every time he had a fight with his wife he immediately used to dress up and go out of the house. His wife though kept on explaining to the other members of the house that she was not guilty.

Haru uncle on that day did not turn up for his lunch even. That was however unnatural because he always used to come back to the house for lunch even though he had tiffs with his wife. My father got back on that day a bit early. Haru uncle did not come by evening also and everyone got tensed a bit. It was 10 o'clock at night and we decided to have our dinner. The other family had also their dinner but Protima aunty kept waiting for his husband's arrival. It was a typical hot and humid summer night in Kolkata. We could not get any sleep and moreover Haru uncle did not come which built a bit of tension amongst us although we knew that he might have been to any of his friend's house as he had a lot of friends in Kolkata. We all gathered together in the open space as we could not get any sleep and sat down to have a chat amongst each other. There was suddenly a noise of the knocking at the main door fiercely. We assumed that Haru uncle might have come and my mother ordered me to open the door but to my amazement there was no one when I had opened the door. I peeped out further into the lane but could not find anyone. Even the stray dogs were also not there in the lane. The lane was completely desolate. I closed the door and came back to my mother frightened about the incident. Everyone seemed to be a bit disturbed by that happening. My father said that someone might have knocked on the door and ran away to have fun. No sooner did my father say those words than the knocking happened again. That time my father went up to see who it was playing the mischief but to no avail. There was no one again. My father asked Raju uncle to climb up the stairs and keep an eye at the lane. He closed the door and kept on standing by it. After a minute's break there came another fierce knock on the door and my father in no time opened it to find no one again. Raju uncle also did not see anyone in the lane. Everyone started to tremble with fear. My father also got a bit confused but to make things a bit easy he claimed that it could be due to sudden winds. However no one was ready to buy that explanation of his as the leaves of the trees were completely still indicating no trace of any breeze even. We all then went back to our respective rooms and decided to ask for an explanation of such unnatural things and sounds that we heard from the land-lady the next morning. We spent the night sleeplessly as those incidents were too shocking for us to digest.

Haru uncle came back early in the next morning and we all asked him where he was the whole day and night in a horrified manner. He replied that he was at his friend's residence at Shyambazar. Looking at our faces he inquired us of what had happened and we narrated the incidents that had happened the previous night. He did not seem to be well convinced with the narration which must be because he did not himself experience the incidents but still went on with us to ask for an explanation from the land-lady. We had all surrounded the land-lady to compel her to speak but she was in no mood to give an explanation. She completely denied that those kinds of incidents could occur though she looked a bit nervous and seemed to hide something from us. We could do nothing much and hence resumed our normal activities. During the afternoon I felt someone else was walking alongside with me wherever I went and that was not only my feeling but everyone else felt the same way when I told that feeling of mine to others. It was not the matter of only one person's feelings, it was felt by everyone. After darkness plunged, from that very day we started hearing cries and a boyish voice weeping continuously. The sound of whipping someone could also be clearly heard from every nook of the house. The sounds of running up and down the stairs of two persons could be well heard and clearly understood but no one could be seen and finally the ultimate day came. The date was 26th of May. The year is not clear in my mind but I can still very well remember the date.

The day was calm but as usually hot and humid. Nothing could be heard on that day. No cries, no sound of whipping and everything seemed to be natural on that day. The unnatural things normally started from the afternoon but on that day everything seemed to have resumed to normal. The sun had gone down and slowly darkness plunged. We all had switched on the lights in our rooms and were happy that nothing unnatural happened on that day. It was 10 o'clock at night. On that day also my father had returned home a little early and since everyone was in the house the main door was closed. Suddenly the lights went off. We assumed that it was load-shedding but all other houses had electricity. Even the street lights were also glowing.

Our house only had plunged into darkness. Candles were lit up as in those days there were no emergency lights, inverter, generator, etc. My father went on to check if the fuse was alright. He saw that the fuse was perfectly alright and therefore we had no clue about why electricity had gone off from our house only. We gathered in the open space in our house so that we could get some breeze outside but we were sweating profusely as there was no trace of any breeze. My mother was sitting on the stairs. Suddenly the sound of whipping started and the voice of a boy could be heard wailing and crying for mercy. The sound was coming down from upstairs by the stairs slowly. My mother felt the sounds of whacking falling just beside her. The cries were close to my mother's ears but there could be seen no one in the lights emitted from the candles. My mother came down from the stairs screaming in fear. The sound of two persons running up and down was heard and even some shadows could also be seen of two persons running up and down the stairs, one of a boy and the other of a large stout woman. We wanted to get out of the house but on approaching the door we found that the door was locked from outside also. We got frightened even further. Both of them were seen running up and then; down came a thudding sound. Suddenly everything stopped and after a minute or two the sound of wailing started. It was 12 o'clock by that time. All sounds vanished after sometime. We did not wait any long. We went to the land-lady's room knocking on the door but there was no sound from her. We all knocked on the door fiercely but there was still no reply from her. The electricity came back and then we decided to go back to our rooms since we got no reply from the land-lady but were determined to force her to speak about those unnatural happenings in the next morning.

There was however no more sound during the night. In the morning we were all still awake as we could not get any sleep after that horrific incident the other night. We wasted no time and went up to the land-lady's room again and started knocking on the door. We were also surprised to find that the land-lady was still sleeping as she was an early riser. We did not get any response from her after knocking several times. We then decided to call the police because we needed to break into the room to check what had happened. The police arrived and with the help of the police we broke into the room to find the body of the land-lady lying dead on the bed in a horrific manner. She seemed to have strangled herself by pressing her throat on her own. The tongue of her was hanging out to her chest. The eyes of her were dilated. It looked as if her eyes were coming out. No one could look at that very sight of her and I was immediately taken to my room by my mother. My mother did not want me to see that view but I had already by that time taken a glimpse. The body was taken for post-mortem and police started to inquire us all about her. We understood that police would not believe our tale about the unnatural happenings and so everyone tactfully avoided to mention about the unnatural happenings. The post-mortem report concluded that she had strangled herself to death which was totally weird.

My mother was not at all ready to stay in the house anymore. She told my father to look for a new house immediately. The news of the death of the land-lady spread like a wild-fire in our area. A Muslim woman in the locality then conveyed the history associated with the house to my mother. Our land-lady had a daughter and a grandson as well. The boy was around eleven years of age. Everything was normal in the beginning but the mother of the boy got involved with some evil tantriks (people who could perform black magic as well) and thereafter problems started to happen. The boy did not like the presence of the tantriks in the house and often protested and he was tortured for that reason. Sacrifices of various forms used to take place in the house. Our land-lady also got involved with them. She also did not protest against those things. One day the boy threatened to go to the police and narrate the whole thing to them and then the torture on the boy became even more severe. Two years ago on that very day when our land-lady died the boy was found dead. Police were called and the woman narrated that the boy had slipped and fallen down from upstairs but it was believed by the people in the locality that the mother had thrown the boy down from upstairs to death. The police got managed and no further investigation was done by them. One year after, on that very day the boy's mother got killed in the same manner as our land-lady. The incident which we experienced was in the second year of the very same date. The thudding sound which we heard on that day may be of the sound of the falling of the boy from upstairs. The deaths might have occurred for revenge. That experience still haunts me from my childhood days. We however shifted from the house immediately in the evening as we had got another place to stay as tenants. All the tenants left the house after that. Haru uncle and his wife only dwelled in that house because they thought that there were no land-lords or land-ladies of the house anymore left to claim for their rents.

They found a way to reduce their cost of living. We never kept any contact with the house anymore and never even tried to go again to the house to check what happened after we had left.

After several years my mother met Haru uncle's wife on the road and heard that Haru uncle was no more. Haru uncle had died drowning in the Deshbandhu Park's swimming pool in spite of being a good swimmer. After her husband's death she also left the house and was staying at her paternal residence.

House at Moulali

[Based on a story which is claimed to be true]

Mr. Piyush Sadhukhan was a pretty rich person in Kolkata. He was the owner of several oil mills near the R.G. Kar Medical College Hospital. He always knew that prices of land properties would always rise and hence purchased whatever houses there was on offer for sale. Likewise he purchased one house at Moulali. After purchasing the house he got to know the history associated with the house.

He heard that the house was haunted. It belonged to a Muslim family in the beginning. During the riots in Bengal this family had to leave the house but a woman stayed there to look after the house. She thought that she would be spared as she was a lady and more so it was their ancestral house and hence she was very much emotionally attached. However that was not the case. She was killed in the house but her body was not found. Ever since that day her soul was heard to roam around in the house. Many people who were very brave and did not believe in ghosts, tried to spend a night in the house but the next day they were found to have become mad. It was said that either the lady was seeking revenge or she was so much emotionally attached to the house that she did not want anyone to dwell in the house other than her. However Mr. Piyush Sadhukhan did not believe in those rumours but he did not dwell in the house as well. Buying houses was just like a business to him which earned him higher profits on his investment after some years.

One day Mr. Piyush Sadhukhan visited a friend's house at Ripon Street. They chatted for hours and had drunk a lot. It was already eight o'clock at night and during those times eight o' clock meant quite late in the night. Buses and taxis used to ply less at night. Mr. Sadhukhan was offered to stay at his friend's residence but he refused and said that he would like to check his Moulali's house which he had purchased recently. Moulali was about twenty minutes walking distance from his friend's residence at Ripon Street. So he set out for his Moulali's residence. Though he was drunk, he was not staggering at all. It was his routine quota of four pegs. After walking for about twenty minutes, he finally reached his destination. The little dizziness that was there, that too was gone after his long walk.

He opened the door with the key and lit all the lights in the rooms. The rooms were all dusty and hence he chose the study room to stay which was more or less clean enough. However he cleaned the room a bit more. Mr. Sadhukhan was fond of books. He used to read a lot and took out one book from the shelf and started to read through it. Suddenly the sound of the clock striking nine echoed in the entire house. Mr. Sadhukhan panicked on the sound of the clock initially but later realized it was the huge pendulum clock on the wall. Fifteen minutes passed, nothing happened but just after that the door of the study room slowly opened up on its own. Mr. Sadhukhan shockingly saw a Muslim lady in a burqah standing in front of the door. She stepped inside the room and walked up to the study table. She drew out a book from the shelf and started reading it. Mr. Sadhukhan could not even blink and stared at the lady for hours. It was at midnight when she closed the book and kept it again in the same place and left the room. Mr. Sadhukhan watched the door of the study room getting closed on its own from inside. He got very much afraid and could not sleep the entire night. In the morning, he started to hear the voice of the lady doing her riyaaz on some Hindustani Classical raga with a tanpura but could be seen nowhere. He then slowly crept out of the house believing there exists if not ghosts then souls. After that day Mr. Sadhukhan did not ever visit that house.

One day Mr. Sadhukhan met a person named Mr. Sujoy Chatterjee at a Hatibagan tea shop. That person was very brave and had worked in the Indian Army for quite a number of years. On their discussions, Mr. Sadhukhan told him about that house of his at Moulali. Mr. Chatterjee did not believe his words and told him that he might have got too intoxicated on that day to see those things that got rooted in his subconscious mind due to the rumours he had heard previously. Mr. Sadhukhan then offered Mr. Chatterjee that if he spent a night in that house then he would gift the house to Mr.Chatterjee. Mr. Chatterjee being a very brave person accepted the offer.

The following evening Mr. Chatterjee met Mr. Sadhukhan at Moulali at seven o'clock. He was taken to the house but Mr. Sadhukhan did not enter the house. Mr. Chatterjee told him to lock from outside if he had any doubts that he would run away after he entered the house. Mr. Sadhukhan did so and went to his friend's residence at Ripon Street to spend the night.

Mr. Chatterjee entered the house and lit all the lights of every room. To ensure that no one else was in the house, he searched every corner of the house. He also searched for any audio-visual aids that could be used for scaring people away from the house. Finding nothing, he went to that study room as told by Mr. Sadhukhan. Here also he checked the room thoroughly. He also checked all the books but he found nothing. He came across a diary in the book-shelf. The diary was written in Urdu. Mr. Chatterjee knew to read Urdu as he had spent several years in Lucknow and had a liking to Urdu poetries. He started to read the diary.

The diary was of the lady named Fatima. It was her personal diary and she had written about her life. The diary told how she was brought up. During that time women were not allowed to go in any school. Education, music, etc. were a strict no for them but her father was against those. Though her father could not violate the rules of the society, he taught music and gave whatever little education he possessed to his daughters. Fatima was very much inclined to study. Mr. Chatterjee was going through the diary when the clock suddenly struck nine. Mr. Chatterjee thought that it was time according to Mr. Sadhukhan. He kept an eye constantly on the door of the study room.

Just at the strike of fifteen minutes past nine, the door started to open up slowly on its own. Mr. Chatterjee had a chill run down by his spine at the look of the lady in the burqah. The lady entered the room and walked up to the same study table; took out a book from the shelf and started reading it. Mr. Chatterjee again regained his courage and asked her what she wanted. He went out from the bed in the study in which he was lying and approached towards the study table. He again asked her but in vain. He then approached his hand towards her to check that if anyone was playing the fool with him. No, he could not feel anyone. He then asked her again to let him know that if he could help her somehow. At that remark of his, the lady turned her face to look at him. Mr. Chatterjee however could not see her face as her face was under the veil. She got up from the chair and Mr. Chatterjee stepped back a few steps. She raised her hand up slowly and indicated by the movement of her hand to follow her. Mr. Chatterjee started to follow her with a bit of fear gripping him. The lady went out of the room and headed towards the stairs to go down. Mr. Chatterjee stepped out of the room and stopped. The lady again turned back and indicated him to come along with her. The lady was going down by the stair-case. Mr. Chatterjee followed her. The lady suddenly stopped in the middle of the courtyard. The courtyard was chequered. She pointed to a crowbar lying against a pillar of the house and instructed Mr. Chatterjee to dig up the middle of the courtyard where she was standing.

Mr. Chatterjee went up to the pillar and picked up the crowbar. He came to the place as indicated by the lady. He pulled out the black and white marbles one by one with the help of the crowbar and then started to dig up the place. After digging up for fifteen minutes or so, he found a skeleton. He immediately looked up to the lady in the burqah. She indicated to say farewell by her gestures and vanished. Mr. Chatterjee stood there spell-bound for about an hour. Then he sat beside the skeleton and examined that the skeleton was of a woman. He waited for sunrise and Mr. Sadhukhan's arrival.

Mr. Sadhukhan arrived early in the morning and almost fainted at the sight of the skeleton in his courtyard. He however regained consciousness and was briefed about what had happened the previous night by Mr. Chatterjee. Mr. Chatterjee and Mr. Sadhukhan sat for a while thinking about what to do with the skeleton. Initially they thought of calling the police but later decided against it because it would cause a lot of problems and harassment for them. They were sure that the skeleton was that of the lady in the burqah and might have been murdered during riots and an investigation would not be helpful except some harassment to them. So they decided to go to their Muslim friend, Hasan and narrate the whole story to him. They decided to bury the skeleton according to

Muslim rituals and prayed so that her soul might rest in peace.

Mr. Sadhukhan gifted the house to Mr. Chatterjee as promised earlier and from that day onwards they believed in spirits and souls. After that no unnatural things ever happened in that house.

Canal Street

[Based on a story which is claimed to be true]

It is a story associated with the house at Canal Street in Kolkata. I have heard it several years before from the owner of the house. I cannot even recall his name as I was very small at that time. I used to study at The Frank Anthony Public School at Ripon Street and after school I used to go along with my father at his party office at Creek Row. He used to have his political discussions and I used to complete my homework in the party office. It happened that that land-lord once came in that party office; I do not know the reason why. He was talking about something when he suddenly started to talk about the unnatural events that used to happen in his house every Saturday. As a young boy, I quickly got interested.

The house previously belonged to a British family. The family comprised of only three members, man, his lady and their only son. The family lived happily before a tragedy happened. Their only son happened to fall in love with a girl who had ditched him one day. He went into depression for quite some days and then suddenly on one Saturday evening committed suicide. Both the parents received a severe shock from their son's death and they also committed suicide, failing to soak in the pain of their son's demise. From that very day, every

Saturday they returned to their son's room to see him and mourn over his death.

That room had many antique furniture worth around a crore of rupees. Many people did not believe in ghosts and he offered that if anyone spent a Saturday night in that room, he would give all the furniture in the room to him. One police officer agreed to do so but he said that he would keep his revolver with him. The landlord agreed to his proposal and one Saturday evening he went to spend a night in that room.

The room had a nice fire place, an arm-chair, a gorgeous bed, and very costly wooden wardrobes, sofa sets, a study table, etc. The police officer went to relax on the bed but after that what happened could not be known properly as he was found unconscious in the next morning and had become mad. The things that could be framed and understood by some of his words were that the lady and his man had come in the room. The lady was threatening him to kill him when he started to fire from his revolver. The lady in reply told him that bullets would do no harm to her as she was not human and after that he collapsed. His revolver was also found empty and seemed that he really did fire from his revolver.

The next was that of another person who was extremely brave and was willing to spend a Saturday night in that room after that incident to see if really ghost existed or not. He came the next Saturday night and went on to the bed to rest. The next day he was found unconscious but he did not become mad. He recovered from a severe shock however for about a week later and then described what had happened on that night.

He said that it was around half past seven in the evening. He was going through the newspaper in the bed when suddenly the arm-chair started moving forward and backward. The door did not open but it sounded like the door was opening (the sound of the hinges). Though it was summer, the fire place lit up on its own. He was startled by those sudden occurrences when suddenly two shimmering figures entered the room. The figures seemed very much like that of the British lady and her man. They were wailing and walked up to the arm-chair. It seemed that their son had committed suicide in the arm-chair but his figure could not be seen. Then suddenly the lady turned towards him and got furious to see him sitting on the bed. He was then struck with immense fear. The lady said to him, "What are you doing in my son's room and on his bed? You have no right to enter in this room without permission." The man then rose up and ordered his lady to kill him. The lady approached towards him slowly to kill him by catching hold of his throat but it was his own hands that were clutching his throat. He tried a lot to control his hands but in vain. His hands were following the instruction of the lady and not his when he lost his consciousness.

Since then the room was kept under lock and key and his house had also got a bad name as haunted house. I do not know what happened to the house after that.

Planchette

[Based on a story which is claimed to be true]

Super-natural things always thrilled my maternal grand-father a lot. My grand-father's father used to read a lot of books and of all kinds such as science, literature, spiritualism, history, geography, wildlife and even astrology, palmistry, numerology, etc. He used to gather knowledge in all subjects and from that collection of books my grand-father also used to read books of his interest. It was from those books that he came to know about planchette. My grand-father's father had a lot of friends from the Theosophical Society as he was also a member of that society and they used to come to his house quite often to discuss about various matters. One day my grand-father overheard his father's discussions with his friends about calling spirits to the material world by means of a planchette. That got my grand-father interested a lot and he crept on close to the door to hear the discussion clearly.

My grand-father's father mentioned the requirements of a planchette and was telling them how it was possible to bring back the spirits of dead people in the present material world for a short duration of time. He said that they would require a person who had a light Zodiac sign like Libra, Pisces, etc. The person would act as a medium through which the spirit could be called down into. As a spirit does not have any form which means after death the spirit loses the bodily structure, a medium of another person's body was therefore required to get the bodily structure. The Zodiac sign of the person to be made the medium should be light because a spirit cannot enter into a person with a powerful Zodiac sign. The spirit can dwell in that body for only a short duration of time as the spirit is too light to stay for longer period in the material world. The conversation with the spirit however could be made through the planchette. Five persons were required to join hands together along with the person who would be made the medium and concentrate very powerfully on the dead person to be called for. He also however mentioned the dangers associated if any evil spirit got into the medium. If any evil spirit gets into the medium, it does not want to leave the medium as it is stronger than other spirits. Evil spirits are the spirits of dead persons who were involved with wrong or criminal activities during their life-time. They actually do not want to leave the material world and thereby can cause even death to the medium.

My grand-father's father's friends however all agreed to conduct it though they had already heard of the risks. The main risk was of the medium but the lady agreed to take the risk because she found that to be a thrilling experience and check whether those things really happened or not. The lady had the Zodiac sign of Libra. They decided to perform the activity at a house at Beadon Street in Kolkata. The house was of one of my grand-father's father's friend's house and there dwelled no one. My grand-father also overheard the date, time and venue clearly and was determined to check the activity of calling spirits himself. He however did not tell anything to his father because he was sure if his father came to know about his visiting the place, he would have cancelled the plan immediately.

My grand-father was a college student at that time and left a bit early for the venue where the activity of calling spirits would be held telling that he had some extra classes and might be late even. He would have to search for the house in the locality as he had never been to the place before and moreover he had to find a place for hiding as well before his father and friends arrived. He found the house and waited opposite to the house for their arrival. After sometime they arrived and went upstairs into the house. My grand-father followed them stealthily into the house. He saw them enter into a room and closed the door. He crept up to the door and peeped through a tiny hole on the door into the room.

The room was dusty and it was very evident that no one used to live in the house for months. The very surroundings within the house were a bit haunted. It was a huge house and was kept locked for some months. However they all sat down on the chairs around a round table. There they placed the planchette board. That was the medium to be used for the conversation with the spirits. They decided to call the spirit of a person who had died just five days ago. That was another point of calling spirits. It is said that calling spirits of persons who died just some days ago is easier than calling the spirits of persons who had died long ago.

Candles were lit up in the room. The electric bulbs and tube-lights were switched off in the room and hence that was the only source of light in the room. My grand-father's heart started pumping faster than ever before but held on to his nerve as he was being driven by his determination to experience it himself rather than anything else. Everybody performing the activity, joined hands and closed their eyes. They started to concentrate hard on the spirit of the dead person and were calling him by his name. After almost ten minutes all the candles in the room suddenly blew off without any trace of wind except for the candle burning at the centre of the table. The lady who was made the medium fell unconscious and her hands were slowly covering up with more hair. Her hands were actually turning up as the hands of a man. The lady started to develop moustaches and beards as well. She was not at all looking fine and her voice changed dramatically. It sounded neither like that of a man nor of a lady but two voices were coming out of her at the same time. My grand-father got the shock of his life on that day. The lady could not however speak in words. My grand-father's father then started questioning if it was the person whom they were calling for. The pencil of the planchette started to move on its own and scribbled through answering in the negative. He then asked for the person's name and the pencil again scribbled on its own to give a name. He questioned him further whether he had any relation with the person whom they were calling for. The pencil again scribbled telling that he was his friend. It again scribbled stating his discomfort in the material world and all the candles lit up on its own again in the room. The spirit was gone. The lady was still lying unconscious and slowly everything resumed to normal. She was made conscious by the other members by sprinkling water on her face. My grand-father then leaped out of the house, half-frightened on what he had experienced and other half of getting caught.

However he still cherishes that experience of his. He tells that had he not gone to experience that, he would have regretted it in his whole life because after that his father never again tried to call down the spirits in the material world and have any conversation with them.

Bardhaman Rajbari

[Based on a story which is claimed to be true]

Bardhaman Rajbari, the palace of Bardhaman, a place in West Bengal. It was the plan of my grandfather and two of his office colleagues to do a picnic at the Rajbari. My grandfather was an employee in the higher rank at the Writer's building and it was easy for him to get the permission to do picnic at the Rajbari. The family members were also going along with them as it was not an office picnic.

Before the day of the picnic, everyone had a meeting and everything was finalised as who was to bring what. Torch, candles, lamps, etc. were the most necessary items. In the morning they all met at the Howrah station and waited for the train to take off. The train finally set off for Bardhaman. After about two and a half hours of journey they reached Bardhaman station. They all took rickshaw and headed for the Bardhaman Rajbari. After reaching there the rickshaw puller exclaimed with dissatisfaction that his day would not go well as they had visited that place. However everyone did not pay any heed to his remarks. They paid him off and he immediately went out quickly from the spot.

The Rajbari was a huge one. At the bottom of the building there were cages where hungry tigers were kept. The Zamindars used to throw their subjects who could not pay taxes into those cages. The tigers were freed from the cages and the Zamindars used to watch the hunt by the tigers for their pleasure. Everyone was thrilled at the look of the palace. So many histories were attached to each and every brick of the Rajbari.

They all started to get inside the palace. All the utensils, oven, vegetables, rice, etc. were arranged by the women while the men were making the candle-stands ready before darkness. My grandfather and his colleagues started to explore the entire Rajbari. They saw the gallows where thieves, criminals and other people whom the Zamindars felt guilty were hanged. The place was however very dusty and the ropes were also torn. They also saw the huge Naach Mahal where the dancers and singers everyday used to gather to entertain the Zamindars. If the Zamindars were pleased with their performance, they used to get rewards or else they were punished severely.

The huge bedrooms were cleaned and everyone chose their respective bedrooms. The lunch was ready and everyone had it satisfying their hunger after a long wait. After a bit relaxation they all set out to explore the palace again. They saw the prisons, battle-training grounds, paintings, swords, etc. My mother was very young at that time and was hence amazed to see the swords that were used during fights. After exploring the palace thoroughly, they lit all the candles at every corner of the palace making the palace full of light. The women again started to cook for dinner and the men sat down and started chatting. Some of them were playing cards and some were helping the women to cook. Dinner consisted of mutton, rice, dal and some fries. My grandfather played cards as he was a master in that game and passionate as well. Dinner was ready by half past eight at night and they decided to complete having it by nine o'clock. After dinner they sat down chatting for half an hour and finally went into their respective bedrooms. My mother was already asleep as the day was too tiring for her at that age.

Things seemed to be normal until midnight. Someone started to laugh in my mother's voice but she was soundly asleep. My grandfather and grandmother both took notice of her but it was not her. The sound was loud enough for everyone to be heard. The sound of the ghungroo (ankle bells) was heard clearly. It was sounding as if someone was dancing along with a song based on Raga Malkauns. The sound was heard to be coming from the same Naach Mahal. Everyone got awake and huddled together. The men decided to check that out while the women stayed together in a room. The Naach Mahal was opened but to their amazement there was none and the sound was also gone. The sound of cries of people in the gallows started to come and the gallows seemed to be working. They rushed towards the gallows but there was none. The knot was just hung up. My grandfather then thought that it might be some miscreants who were trying to frighten them when suddenly a cold wind came from nowhere blowing out all the candles in the palace at one go. The palace became pitch black dark. They took out their torches when suddenly the roaring of the tigers started and a voice of ordering people to do something was heard prominently. It sounded as that of a Zamindar. The cries of many people reverberated in the whole palace. The sound of whipping people and their cries filled the whole palace. The new battery operated torches suddenly stopped functioning and they all rushed back to their rooms. They all just waited for the night to get over. All doors were locked properly from inside and spent a sleepless night hearing many sounds.

Just before dawn the mosquito nets seemed to be pulled down by someone forcibly indicating the people to leave the palace immediately. However they had all waited till sunrise and then immediately packed their bags and set out for home realising the truthfulness in the rickshaw-puller's words.

No one said anything to anyone about the things that had happened on that night as people would not have believed them and might have even considered them as mad.

Divine Existence

[Based on a story which is claimed to be true]

It was a case in a village named Palong in Madaripur sub-division of Faridpur district in Bangladesh. At that time, Bangladesh was in India only and it was only Bengal. Thousands of people used to die from small pox as there was no cure from it during those days.

That village was also hit by the virus and thousands were dying from small pox. The Mukhuty family were the Zamindars of the village and the Pujas were all organized by that family for the welfare of the village. The Durga Puja of the Mukhuty family was a renowned one.

The women of the Mukhuty family started fasting and praying in front of the Durga temple for protecting their family and village from small pox. After five consecutive days of fasting they all had a vision of a way to save the lives of the people. It was some unknown power that gave them that vision. They went back to their home and saw that their family had also got affected by small pox. Three of them stayed back to serve their family members while the two elder wives of the family set out as they saw in their vision.

They went to their corresponding village and found the pond. The old dilapidated temple was the only thing that was there as the place was totally deserted. They both entered into the temple and found the wooden stairs. It was a temple of Lord Shiva. They crept down the stairs and found three tunnels. They decided to go together and chose one tunnel. It was pitch black dark inside. One of them tore away a piece of her saree and made torchlight. Weeds were growing all over and poisonous snakes were all around. They however progressed through the tunnel taking the name of Lord Shiva and to their amazement the snakes moved out.

After walking for five minutes through the tunnel, they found the exit. There was a huge lake and all the exits of the tunnel eventually ended up there. The old dilapidated house could also be seen near the lake as they saw in their vision. It was the house of a Hindu priest during the Mughal emperor Akbar's time. They entered the house and found the broken wooden almirah. They opened it and found the ancient book wrapped in a red shawl. As the eldest housewife took it up in her hands, conch and bells started ringing from nowhere. In those days women in India were not supposed to read and write and hence they quickly took it to their home.

Their family priest was called and he said that it was the book of Goddess Swetala's Puja's norms. He asked them to arrange all the requirements that were stated in the book for the Puja and Yajna. The Puja then started at the Durga temple only. During the Puja he made a mistake in the pronunciation of a certain mantra and immediately gusts started to occur from nowhere at the temple only. The bells of the Durga temple were ringing at very high decibels. The priest understood his flaw and started the Puja again from the beginning very cautiously.

After the Puja was complete, dark clouds gathered only in their village and it started to rain gently for three consecutive days. All the people in that village got cured from small pox and no one died of it from the time the book was taken in the hands of the eldest housewife of the Mukhuty family.

It is said that the vaccine of small pox was discovered after that Puja only and the entire world got benefited from that Puja.

The Case of Khardah

[Based on a story which is claimed to be true]

It was during the 1980s when the incident had happened. In those days Khardah was not well developed and it had only a very few families who dwelled over there. People who mainly came from Bangladesh as refugees, settled at that place. It was an incident that happened with the Saha family. Hori was a notorious chap of the Saha family and he used to disturb everyone at Khardah. He was the mastermind of playing pranks on people. He was so disturbing that his family members were also disgusted with him. One day, he drowned in the biggest pond at Khardah as he tried to swim though he did not know how to. After three days his body was recovered from the pond and his last rites were completed according to Hindu shastra. The residents of Khardah were in fact very happy with his tragic death. Nothing unusual happened for the following few days.

Bengalis, especially the people of Bangladesh are very fond of fish and it was during the monsoons, the time of relishing the Hilsa. Hori's favourite was also Hilsa and it happened that the Saha family decided to have Hilsa. Raju uncle, the head of the Saha family was returning from his office and bought a Hilsa on his way back. He used to return through the graveyard as it was a shortcut way to his home.

He was carrying the fish in his right hand humming a Kishore Kumar's very popular song. It was nine o'clock at night and no one used to be there near the graveyard at night. Moreover since very few people lived at Khardah during those days, everyone preferred to stay indoors after the sunset. Suddenly he started hearing the sound of footsteps following him through the graveyard. He stopped immediately and turned back but there was none in sight. He again started walking and again the footsteps were following him and it got very close to him. He turned back and again there was none. He tried to dismiss all the thoughts that were evolving but it was actually clogging his mind more and more. He started to walk at a faster pace and the footsteps also followed him at a faster pace. He stopped and turned again but that time there was a huge roar of laughter that echoed in the entire graveyard. The laughter was that of Hori and there was none in sight.

Raju uncle quickly returned back to their house and told not to cook the fish. He told his wife to burn the fish. His wife got very upset as Hilsa is always a costly fish. He then explained what had happened. His wife again got even more upset as she got frightened if something would have happened with her husband. The actual problems started to occur from the following day.

The next morning Raju uncle was ready to go to his office. As he was about to leave, he felt that someone pushed him with tremendous force from behind. He could not keep his balance and fell down hurting himself severely. He was bleeding profusely as his nose broke and lips got cut. He could not go to office that day as he had to be taken to the hospital for first-aid. Everything resumed to normal after that incident until after two weeks. It was raining on that night. Raju uncle as usual came back home from office at night. He got fresh and sat down for his dinner. His dinner was served by his wife and suddenly from nowhere latrine of that of a man dropped on his food. Both he and his wife got frightened and that roar of laughter echoed in the entire room. Both of them huddled together with fear and spent the whole night in shock.

Fear gripped them completely after that. Every inch they moved, they moved in fear that something evil might happen. Doors and windows opened and closed automatically. Every day Hori's voice and laughter could be heard. One night while Raju uncle's wife was serving dinner to him, she stopped suddenly. She closed her eyes and shook her head with great pace. At that sight, Raju uncle got spell-bound. She opened her eyes after a while. Her voice changed completely. Her eyes were as red as hibiscus. She looked straight at Raju uncle and said, "I am not your wife now. I am Hori. I am unable to leave the material world and hence I need your help. I don't want to cause any harm to anyone. As my death is not natural I could not get out of the material world. You need to go to Gaya and do *pind daan.* It is only after that I can get out of the material world." Raju uncle was struck with fear but managed to ask somehow, "How will I understand after *pind daan* that you have got relief from the material world?" She replied, "I stay on that mango tree at the backyard. When you will complete the *pind daan,* a branch of the tree will break down and you will know that I have got relief from the material world." Soon after that word Raju uncle's wife became unconscious. When she regained consciousness, she seemed to be normal but did not remember any part of the incident that had happened during that phase.

The next day Raju uncle set out for Gaya. He wanted to complete the *pind daan* as soon as possible. As he completed the *pind daan,* one branch of the mango tree broke down on its own. It was only after that everything resumed to normal and never anything of that sort happened ever after. The only very few old people of Khardah who witnessed that incident still recall even today.

Weird Magic

It was in the lands of Assam, a state in India where this incident happened for about ninety years ago. There was a tribe in a very remote area of Assam and those areas were strictly forbidden to enter for the outside world. Those areas were barricaded and military personnel used to maintain the vigilance.

It happened that a person named Sajal went to his relatives' homes in Assam. He was from Bangladesh but at that time it was all India. Sajal was a dark complexioned but handsome person. He was an acrobatic as well as an adventurous person. He used to travel to different places in Assam while residing in his relatives' homes. One day he decided to go to the remote areas of Assam though he was warned by his relatives. In the morning he set off and went to the remote area which was barricaded. There was a board hanging; displaying "Prohibited Area". He approached the military personnel and asked them about the place. They replied that the area had been prohibited because tribal people used to dwell in that area and they did not like to get disturbed by the outside world and might cause harm to the outside world on any intrusion. That reply was enough to make Sajal more curious about the tribal people and the place. He decided to return back on that day and chalk out a plan to slip through the barricade.

The military personnel employed on vigilance were low. The barricade was of iron fence which he could easily climb over. The only thing was to distract the military personnel for about a few minutes so that he could climb over.

The next day he went there again. Hiding himself cleverly, he gathered some dry leaves and lit them up. Seeing a fire and smoke, the two military personnel got distracted and went forward to check that out. Meanwhile Sajal had ample time to climb over the barricade. He landed in the zone of the tribal people. He ran deep inside through the jungle and finally saw some tent-like huts. He saw females of different ages cooking food, making clothing of their kinds, etc. He thought that the males might have gone for farming but later in the evening he saw that some females only returned from somewhere.

He decided to have a few words with them and hence approached towards them. On seeing him, they were taken aback at first and then quickly a few ladies pounced on him with their spears. They tied his hands. He tried to make them understand that he meant no harm to them but to no avail. He was taken to an old lady, probably the chief of their community. She was wearing the nails of tigers around her neck. Her eyes were reddish. She was furious to see him. Everyone in their community had short noses and small eyes. The old lady ordered something in her language which Sajal did not understand but understood that something very bad was going to happen to him. He pleaded that he meant no harm but in vain. A lady standing close to him grasped some burning ashes in her hand. She spelt some verses and threw it on him. Within a second, he found himself that he had become a sheep but could talk in his own voice.

Interestingly his appetite changed as well and he was given grass to eat. While he was eating the grass, he found that the other animals which he thought to be animals were not exactly animals. They were humans but the males. The women used to turn the men into animals according to their choice. The cows, bulls, dogs, cats, etc. were all male humans. The area was dominated by the tribal women. The next day he was taken to the farm to graze. At night, he was given back his self-identity of the man. The lady used to spell some verses and he changed into his self at night. That continued for several years.

On one fine morning, another old lady of the tribe felt pity for him. She said that twelve years had passed. She asked him to climb up on the tallest tree in that area and he did so. The lady then spelt something and he fell down on the courtyard of his residence in Bangladesh.

Everyone in his family was amazed to see him back after twelve years and especially in that manner. Everyone had thought that he might have been dead. He then narrated the entire story that had happened with him.

Goabagan Street

[Based on a claimed to be true story]

When we came to dwell at a house at Goabagan Street, there lived no one in the next house. The house used to remain under lock and key. After three years or so, a family bought the house. Being neighbours, we introduced ourselves and they also introduced themselves to us. We all became friends. The head of the family was Khetra Babu. He was a professor as well as a well-to-do businessman. Their family was a nuclear family and they had a parrot as a pet. In the initial years, everything was fine. Nothing unusual seemed to be there.

On one moonless night, things completely changed ever after. The parrot in the courtyard cried on top of its voice. No one could understand for what it was crying out. The next morning everyone was shocked to see it lying dead; more so in a horrific manner. Blood was spewing all over. The neck of it was broken and wings of it were torn apart and that too within the cage. Everyone went mum for a few days. No one could believe their eyes and figure out how that incident could have happened.

After a few days, Khetra Babu incurred severe losses in his business. That resulted in a major heart attack of Khetra Babu. Though he got saved, his left side got paralysed completely. Two unnatural incidents one after the other created a bit of tension amongst all of us. Two days later, Khetra Babu's wife was found dead on the second floor. It seemed that she had committed suicide as she hanged herself with her saree from the ceiling fan. She almost had no reason to commit suicide as Khetra Babu had enough riches though he had incurred losses. There were no fights in the family and moreover doctors had said that Khetra Babu would get completely cured after two months. After Khetra Babu's wife's death, there was a bit of uneasiness with the building in the locality. Khetra Babu shifted to his ancestral house and kept no contact with us ever since.

After about two years, another family bought the house and came to stay in that house. Since we were neighbours, we became friends with that family as well but did not disclose what had happened previously because we did not want them to get negatively afflicted. That family was also a nuclear family. I can recollect only the lady's name. Her name was Mrinmoyee. I did not like that lady at all as she was very mean-minded and probably that is the reason why I can recollect only her name. Everything was alright with that family as well just like it happened with the previous family. As neighbours we used to go to their house but after a few days we did not seem to be comfortable in that house. The feeling cannot be expressed in words. It seemed like some evil forces did not like our presence in that house, may be because we were Brahmins.

One afternoon, Mrinmoyee was heard crying out with immense fear. We rushed to their house immediately. Mrinmoyee described that she saw a shadow of a lady hanging from the ceiling as she entered the room on the second floor. We all looked at each others' faces. She did not know the history and hence that incident could not be thrown out as her illusion. However we consoled her by saying that it was her illusion though deep in our hearts we knew that something unnatural seemed to be present in that house.

The houses of North Kolkata were built side by side on same walls. Hence all the houses were interconnected through the roofs. One can easily go from one house to another house from the roof-tops. Similarly our house and Mrinmoyee's house were also interconnected.

It was during the time of Vishwakarma Puja when my friend had the shock of his life. We used to fly kites. My friend had come the previous night of Vishwakarma Puja and stayed at my house. We used to fly kites from our roofs. At four o' clock in the morning, he awoke and went up onto the roof to check the direction of the breeze.

As he went up, he saw a lady in a white saree standing on the roof. He called her and she turned towards him. To his shock, he saw the lady was beheaded and approaching towards him. He screamed and leaped down from the roof and called up everybody. Everyone went up to check but the lady was nowhere. The door of the roof of Mrinmoyee's house was also locked.

I was then brought up at my maternal house and hence knew nothing about what had happened later. After several years when I went to visit the house again, I came to know that whoever bought the house had fallen in severe crisis and left the house. It also happened that a person had bought the house and started to renovate it. Some unnatural happenings started to occur and the labourers did not want to work anymore. Moreover after a few days, the landlord had also fallen ill severely. The house still remains under lock and key.

The Dumas Beach

One fine morning Devendra uncle and his wife Minu aunty arrived at our home to give a surprise visit. It was very long since we all got together so it was very exciting and we decided to chill out that entire day. Devendra uncle bought a new Labrador and its name was Tommy. Tommy happened to be very friendly and well trained. I really love pets and so made good friendship with Tommy.

My school's winter vacation was coming close and so we decided to go to Gujarat for our holidays. We also took Tommy with us. Tommy was also excited with holidays as it expressed its happiness by its own means of wagging its tail, licking us, etc. It was a planned tour of ten days. We had completed touring all the tourist spots of Gujarat within seven days. We were all fond of sea-side and hence decided to spend the remaining days at the Dumas beach which is approximately twenty one kilometres away from Surat.

The beach is made of black sand which makes it a mesmerising one and a treat for the eyes. The hotels were however far from the beach. The waves of the Arabian Sea are not huge. It is more or less like a huge sleeping water-body.

We went out on the beach to enjoy the soothing fresh air blowing over the sea but Tommy was barking and howling a lot unnecessarily. It seemed very unnatural as Tommy was a very well mannered dog. After walking some distance on the beach, Tommy started to bark louder and was not ready to move an inch further. We all scolded Tommy to behave properly but in vain. In fact it stopped us from walking further down the beach.

We went back to our hotel. We came back to the sea-shore again at dusk but that time left Tommy in the hotel. I was strolling down alone on the beach when suddenly I heard some whispers in my ears. I stopped and turned back. No one was even near to me. I could not understand from where the whispers could have come. I again resumed strolling. Again I heard the whispers and felt as if someone was standing just beside me but to my astonishment there was none. I went back to my parents in a confused state of mind. We all went back to the hotel together. Everyone felt a bit uneasy but no one told anything to anyone.

The boy in our hotel warned us that we should not go out in the night as it was not a safe place. Devendra uncle said, "Not safe, in what sense?" The boy said, "My duty was to warn you. I will not like to say the reason why." He left immediately.

In spite of being warned, Devendra uncle and Minu aunty went to the sea-side to enjoy the night view after dinner. The next morning we got up and saw that they did not return. We went out to the beach and started to search for them but in vain. We informed the police and registered a missing diary.

Locals said that the beach is a cremation ground for the people who died unnatural deaths. Spirits of them hover around and their whispers can be heard. At that word, I was spellbound as I had also heard whispers and felt someone standing beside me though there no one could be seen. Many people disappeared at night and dogs bark and howl often as they can sense the spirits better than man. Hence Tommy's unnatural behaviour on that day was no exception. Devendra uncle and Minu aunty remain missing till today.

Dead Man Crying

The sky above the port changed into a dead channel. The very sight of that gripped everyone present at the port with fear and everyone could view the channel. Blood was dropping from the sky and cries of 'help, save me' were being heard. People could not move an inch; trembling with fear; they were feeling as if someone was clutching their feet tightly. The flashes then came on the sky-turned channel of a dead face crying for help. Storms and thunders started to occur. It became outrageously dark and the dead face was appearing prominently now. Blood was oozing out from his head as his head was half open. He was trying to say something to the people present but they were too frightened to hear a word of his.

Suddenly everything stopped. A movie got started featuring the dead man whose name was mentioned as Raghav. The date was mentioned as July 31, 2009, the same date a year ago. The feature film started showing a dark night, raining heavily accompanied with lightning and thunders. The same port on which everyone was present was under construction at that time. Raghav and Suresh were the contractors of the port. Raghav was mainly the sleeping partner and Suresh was the active partner amongst the two. Suresh looked after the daily progress of the work and used to make the dealings and everything else that an active partner has to do in the business. Raghav had full faith in his partner though he found many flaws with the accounts. Suresh used to take advantage of his partner's full faith in him. He used to steal the materials used for construction and took bribes from the suppliers to sanction the tenders. The continuous stealing of materials from their go-down made Raghav suspicious because there were only two keys of their go- down. Both the partners had their respective keys only and no one else could have them. That growing suspicion made Raghav one night set forth to their go-down to inspect any unscrupulous activity. When he reached there, he found his partner standing and giving orders to some persons to clear some of the stock lying in the go-down. Raghav immediately went on to stop them. The very sight of his partner made Suresh completely perplexed at first but came back to his self again quickly and got involved in a tiff. Suresh then tried to convince Raghav that he would not steal the materials again and wanted him to take his share of the bribes which he used to get by sanctioning the tenders for the supply of the materials but Raghav was a tough nut to crack. He was not at all ready to agree to any unfair means in business. He threatened Suresh that he would go to the police and narrate the whole thing to them. Suresh, seeing no way to escape struck Raghav fiercely on his head with a spade which was lying nearby. His head immediately split half-open and he died immediately in a pool of blood. He was then buried under the workplace of construction itself under a red round symbol.

Vijay, who was a coolie at the port looked down and saw that he was standing on the same red round symbol. A hand was coming out from the ground trying to clutch his leg and voices crying out 'save me' were being heard. Vijay screamed out loudly and everything resumed to normal at once. Everyone was horrified and looked at each other. Voices of 'Help me, Save me' were again heard faintly to assure that it was not a hallucination. Police were summoned and the place was dug up. The body of the dead man was found and police started to investigate into the matter. Suresh was found guilty and got arrested. Raghav's family then performed the obsequies of Raghav's body and his soul then rested in peace.

The Death in the Valley

It was very chilly inside his room. Chat boxes were popping up on its own in his laptop and they all carried the same message, "Go in the valley of death and kill yourself". He was utterly confused by the messages and kept thinking if he actually kept his laptop switched on but to his amazement he could clearly remember of switching off his laptop. He was also thinking of the strange messages that had popped up. He was feeling very cold and so decided to have a cup of coffee in the nearby cafeteria. He went out and found a letter in his letter box making him completely perplexed as he remembered that there was no letter in his letter box when he came back from his office and no one gave delivery of letters during night time. He looked at his watch and saw it was 9 p.m. He opened the letter and found it stating his mother's sickness. He immediately called up his mother but there was no response. He went back to his room and started calling up his mother again but to no avail.

He then immediately decided to pay a visit to his mother's residence because he feared that something might have happened to her. As he approached his car, he remembered of the pop ups and the valley through which he needed to travel in order to go to his mother's residence but his concern for his mother drove him much more than the pop ups. The roads were completely desolate and it looked as if they were staring at him in anger. He was driving his car in full speed. As he entered the valleys, an ominous fear was looming over his head. He felt his heart was beating very fast and could not even breathe properly. Suddenly he saw a man running towards his car wildly. He tried to apply brakes but the brakes were malfunctioning. The man got hit by the car severely and the car automatically stopped. It seemed as if the brakes were not functioning for that accident to occur. He got out of the car and saw his car strewn with blood. He started to look for the man's body but could not find anything. The body had vanished but the road was filled with blood. Turning back he saw a man standing right behind him. He got shocked as if he saw a ghost. The man asked him what had happened but he could not tell anything to him and pointed towards the wheels of his car. Surprisingly there was no blood anywhere. The man then advised him not to stay in the valley for long as evil spirits dwelled in it.

He then hurried up back in his car and the man started laughing out loudly. He then saw his hands, the steering, the seats, and everything inside in his car, drenched with blood. He screamed out loud but the man was nowhere around anymore. His eyes were closing; heart was stopping to pump and was gasping for breath.

The next morning police found his dead body in the car and sent it for post-mortem. The post-mortem report said that he had died of profuse bleeding due to hypertension. When the police went to inform his mother of his death, they found that his mother also died of profuse bleeding due to hypertension in the same night. Co-incidence or something else....

The Station-Master

It was one o' clock at night when the train jerked to a halt at some unknown station. Reena woke up and to her amazement, the compartment was desolate. She peeped out of the window and saw no one at the station. The station had no lights and was pitch black dark. She found that even her mother who was sitting just beside her was not present. She started to feel extremely afraid. She wanted to drink some water but her bottle was empty. She had to get down from the train to fill her bottle.

She could not find any source of water at the station. The station was old and desolate. It seemed as if no train had passed through that station for years. At a distance she could see a candle light. She started to approach towards the light when suddenly she heard some voices whispering just behind her. She turned around immediately and saw no one. She continued moving towards the light and saw that it was the room of the station master. Getting a bit relieved she entered the room but saw no one. The station master was nowhere. An eerie wind blew and the candle light was blown off. The room went totally dark. She turned to run out of there but her feet were not moving. She was feeling like someone was holding her legs tightly. She then heard a voice calling out her name in agony "Reena". She turned behind and saw a very old man in a station master's uniform standing with blood on his shirt and face. She became extremely afraid and wanted to scream out loud but her throat felt like clutched together and could not speak a word.

She got extremely afraid and thought that she might die but the man told her that he was her grandfather. Reena was in no mood to hear his words and wanted to run but the man convinced her of no harm. The man said that he had died in a train accident and was the station master of Burdwan junction. His last wish was to see his grand-daughter and so he did not get nirvana. He said that his soul had waited for fifteen years at the station to meet his grand-daughter. He then gave something in her hand and vanished. Soon after, Reena collapsed.

When she regained her consciousness, she found that the train was at the Burdwan junction and was sitting beside her mother in the train. She found her mother weeping and asked her why she was weeping. Her mother then told the same story of her grand-father which she had already heard from him whom she previously had never seen except in the dream. Reena then opened her fists as there was something and found that it was a locket that her grand-father gave her. She opened the locket and saw that it contained pictures of his grand-father and grand-mother. As she showed it to her mother, she realized that that was the locket which

Reena's grand-father used to wear around his neck. It was not found after the accident of his.

The Story of Balkan Peninsula

It was a lovely fine sunny morning at the Balkan Peninsula. The glaciers on the mountain tops were shining brightly in the sun. There was peace all around and a great feeling of calmness and solitude. Three friends from India came on that very day as tourists. They were spell-bound by the attractive view of the place. Vijay, Raj and Dennis were the three friends. Dennis was actually a native of the Balkan Peninsula but stayed in India because his company transferred him over there. Vijay and Raj were his office colleagues as well as friends. It was Dennis who had decided to spend that time's vacation at his native place with his friends. Vijay and Raj gladly accepted the idea as they had never been to any foreign place.

It was ten past ten in the morning when they had arrived at the place and headed straight to Dennis' home in the village nearby. No one lived at Dennis' home after his mother had expired in the last year. The house was taken care of by Dennis' uncle George and he was informed about their visit well in advance. He had therefore cleaned up the house and made all arrangements for their stay. The breakfast was kept ready for them. On their arrival, they were warmly greeted by Dennis' uncle. They all gorged on the delicious breakfast prepared by Uncle George. After they had their breakfast, they went out for sight-seeing. The hills and the mountains were eye-catching. The meadows were lush green and huge farmlands were being cultivated by the villagers. All of them knew Dennis and everyone greeted him for his arrival. Many of them asked about his stay in India and also inquired him of his Indian friends. They also greeted Vijay and Raj and asked them about how they liked their place.

After walking about a mile over the huge fields, they had reached towards the mountainous range. Dennis had never been to that part of the land. In fact nobody went to that part of the land. The history of the Balkan Peninsula was however unknown to Dennis. They were passing by a hill when they were astounded by a white palace upon the hill which Dennis did not know of. The white palace was a grand one. The gate was made of brass but wild plants grew all around the place making the place look ugly. Climber plants were clinging onto the gate. It seemed that no one had been to that palace for years. Vijay asked Dennis about the history of the palace but he was unaware of it himself. He decided to ask about it to his uncle. After removing some of the climber plants from the gate they found that the gate was bound by a huge iron chain and locked from outside and the Holy Cross was hanging upon the gate. They all thought that the place might be holy but the structure of the palace was not like that which Dennis indicated quickly. They inspected all around the palace but the boundary walls were too high for anyone to climb. The walls were also of white marble but climber plants were hanging from all over providing an eerie look to the palace. The time went beyond two o'clock and Dennis thought that it would get late to reach home if they did not start then. They were also feeling a bit hungry and therefore thought to leave for home immediately.

On the way home Dennis kept on thinking whether to ask about the palace to his uncle or not. They discussed all the way back and finally Dennis agreed to ask about the matter to his uncle because the secrets needed to be revealed. However after reaching home, he quickly changed his mind in the negative and gave the message to his friends about not disclosing the matter to his uncle by the means of signs and gestures. He changed his mind because he realized that they had found an adventurous mystery to solve in his hometown and that could be a thrilling experience in the vacation. Above all, he also realized that that was a village and superstitions might follow if something really sacred was there at that palace. Their going out might be restricted which might mar their enjoyment in the vacation. Post lunch, Dennis went out to the blacksmith's place to get a chisel and a hammer. Vijay and Raj went to get some rest and kept on talking between themselves about the palace and what could the history be behind it in their mother tongue that is in Hindi which Uncle George could not get any hint of. Dennis came back before the sunset and hid the chisel and hammer in the warehouse which was at the back of their home. Dennis and his friends decided to leave early in the next morning and would go straight to the white palace. Dennis informed them that he had bought a chisel and hammer to break the lock of the gate and they were all happy to have a great adventure the next day.

The three friends got up early in the morning and were ecstatic for their adventure. They had their breakfast quickly and informed Uncle George that they might not return in the afternoon and would therefore buy bread and butter from the nearby shop on their way which they would have for lunch. Dennis quickly went out to the warehouse and took the chisel and the hammer along with him and set forth towards the palace. After walking about an hour or two they finally reached the palace. The lock was a huge one and it was impossible to break it even with a chisel and hammer. Dennis decided to break off the chain by which it was bound. Out of the three, Vijay was well-built and therefore he decided to start the proceedings of cutting the chain. They interchanged the work several times as breaking down the chain was not easy at all. After about two and a half hours of rigorous hammering on the chain, it finally broke. They removed the chain and entered into the premises.

The garden was no more decorated. Wild plants were growing all over. The fountain in the middle of the garden was broken. It looked like a ruined place. They approached towards the main entrance door of the palace when suddenly dark clouds formed from nowhere and were looming all over the sky with thunder and lightning. They opened the door with a screeching sound. It was a shrill sound that hurt the ears of the three. Soon after a group of bats came flying out of the palace. They were taken aback but again started to proceed forward.

It was pitch-black dark inside the palace. The windows were covered up with brown paper and also pieces of wood were nailed all over the windows to block light from entering into the palace. This seemed to be very weird. It was dusty all over and spider's web covered up the interior of the palace completely. It was not possible to open the windows but light was required to check inside the palace. Luckily Raj used to smoke a lot and therefore he used to carry matches with him always lest they should have had to return for that day to go home and bring matches the next day. Raj lit up the matches and took a glimpse all around. He found there were many candle stands around every nook of the palace. Meanwhile it started to rain cats and dogs accompanied by sudden winds which blew off the match-stick. Dennis went towards the door and locked it. Raj lit up another match-stick and went towards the nearest candle-stand and lit that up. Slowly he lit up all the candles in the palace. The interior of the palace was quite visible then. A huge painting of a handsome looking man was hung upon a wall. The frame of the painting was made of pure gold. They all gathered in front of the painting. They were amazed to see it. It was an elegant one and the name of the person was written as "Johan Smith, 1809- ." The date of death was missing from the painting. The present year was 1927 and it was impossible for anyone to be still alive for any person who was born in the year 1809. They assumed that the Royal mansion was of the person in the painting but his whereabouts were unknown. The staircase was also of white marble. It was leading to the upper half of the Royal mansion. They slowly walked upstairs. Raj again lit up the candles that were present upstairs. They advanced towards a room that seemed to be the bed-room of the palace.

That room was also bound by a chain and the Holy Cross was hanging from it. Dennis removed the chain and opened the door of the room and the same screeching sound followed. The room was dark and Raj had to light up the room again. As soon as Raj lit up one of the candle-stands, they got shocked by the presence of a huge coffin upon the bed which was blood stained. The three regained their composure and lit up rest of the candles in the room to inspect the room thoroughly. Nothing was present in the room except the bed stained with blood and upon it the huge coffin. The three huddled together as they got a bit scared and slowly advanced towards the coffin. Vijay, the most courageous of the three started lifting up the cover of the coffin slowly. After the cover was removed they found the same handsome man lying in the coffin with a dagger designed in the form of the Holy Cross pierced through the heart. Dennis removed the dagger and wondered why that person had been murdered. Soon after Raj realised that how a person's dead body had not decomposed after several years of death. The dagger in Dennis' hand fell down on the floor as he got astonished and realised the reality in Raj's comment. They started trembling with fear and ran out of the room immediately.

The rains in the meanwhile had stopped but the sky had still black clouds all over. It was still murky but all three were running through the meadows with their hearts in their mouths. They wanted to reach home as fast as possible. The fields had become muddy and hence slippery. They had slipped during their run towards their home many times and even had fallen to the ground injuring themselves, but they did not care. All their focus at that time was to reach home.

Uncle George was amazed to see their conditions when they reached home at last. He inquired them of what had happened but they concocted a story and told him. They did not reveal to him the true facts that had happened. After dark they all stood in the balcony and discussed the matter when sudden cries came from the village. A huge bat could be seen flying in the night sky. They at once went into their room and closed the doors and windows.

In the morning they went to the village and heard that the vampire was back after several decades and one of them was taken by him the other night. Dennis, Raj and Vijay looked at each other and asked them about the history of the place as it was unknown to Dennis even. The villagers then went on to narrate the history several decades old.

Johan Smith was a person of noble descent and had his palace near the mountains. He was the owner of the entire village and he once went to some place that no one knew of and when he came back, he was completely a changed man. He spoke to no one and kept himself confined to the four walls of his palace only. After one week of his return people started disappearing from the village and a huge bat could be seen flying in the night sky. The villagers got extremely scared and never went out after dark. Once two of the villagers went out in the night because one of them was ill and it was on that very night the mystery behind the villagers' disappearance was revealed. When the two were making their way to the doctor's residence, the bat changed to be Johan Smith and turned into a vampire. His two canine teeth were protruding and pounced upon one while the other somehow managed to escape because he had the locket of the Holy Cross worn around his neck which he thought had saved him. He revealed that incident to the rest of the villagers the next day and soon after to their fortune they saw a young man come riding on horse-back. He gave his identity that he was a vampire slayer and briefed them about the incidents that had occurred when Johan Smith was out of the village. He said that Johan Smith was slightly bitten by a vampire when he found him and thought that treatment could cure him from becoming a vampire and hence initially did so but later on he found in an old book that once bitten, there was actually no cure from becoming a vampire. By that time Johan Smith had come back to his village and had also turned into a vampire. Hence he had come immediately for the rescue of the villagers. That person was the grandfather of Dennis and therefore they were so much respected in the village as he had saved them from the hands of the vampire.

The three after hearing the history of the place went back to their house and confessed their guilt to Uncle George. Uncle George was astonished to hear that they had freed the vampire. He told them that that vampire was not like others. Since he was of noble descent, he could not be killed completely. The cross shaped dagger pierced through his chest, confined him in his coffin for several decades and Dennis' grandfather thus decided to stay in the village thereafter to protect the villagers if somehow the vampire got freed. The old book was taken out from an old chest by Uncle George where the process of combating a vampire was written.

The book said that to combat a vampire of noble descent the Holy water was essential and any normal dagger would not solve the purpose. The dagger should be jewelled and ornamented specially and should be designed in the form of the Holy Cross. The dagger should be pierced right through the vampire's heart lest it should not work. The vampire could only be partly killed during dawn. They realised that it was only that dagger that could solve the purpose and it was their responsibility to save the villagers from the vampire as they had freed him. The three Raj, Vijay and Dennis geared up for their combat with the vampire. Meanwhile Uncle George went to get the Holy water and came back before dark. He also prepared himself to go along with them and set out for the palace before dusk.

The very sight of the palace gave an eerie feeling in all of them but Uncle George was quick to realise to give some motivation and tips to the three. He said that the Holy Cross did not work unless they had the courage and full belief in it. The first thing that they needed to do was to find the dagger in the palace. They entered the palace with the same screeching noise and found the palace lit up by candle-lights. They saw Johan Smith coming down in a silk night gown and welcomed them all to the palace. "Hello Dennis! How are you doing?" Johan Smith said to Dennis. Dennis was shocked to find out that the person or vampire knew his name. Johan Smith went on, "What happened? Are you shocked that I know your name? In fact I know everyone's name over here. Raj and Vijay, you both are from India and Dennis' friends, right?" Uncle George was quick to interrupt, "Will you stop your nonsense?" He turned to the three and warned, "Do not look into his eyes. He can hypnotise you." Johan Smith again started, "Let them decide what they want to do. Why are you interfering in between us? It seems that you are most prepared to die." Dennis replied, "Are you prepared to die Mr. Johan Smith?" Johan Smith replied back, "My death is not possible. Your grandfather was a great vampire slayer but even he could not kill me. What will you do? So you all better surrender before me." Dennis took out the Holy Cross from his pocket but Johan Smith advanced forward and crushed the Cross with his hand. Uncle George immediately warned Dennis about the courage and faith in the Holy Cross and pulled out his Cross from his pocket. Johan Smith slowly started moving back but quickly pounced on Vijay. Vijay was a Brahmin and he started chanting the Gayatri mantra immediately which burnt the vampire partly and it turned into a bat and flew off.

Uncle George was quick to realise the opportunity to find out the dagger. He quickly informed them to show the place where they last left the dagger. They moved up the stairs and entered into the bedroom of the vampire. The coffin was lying on the bed but the dagger was not on the floor where Dennis had last left on getting shocked. They all started to seek for the dagger everywhere. It could not be found. Suddenly Raj stepped on a carpet but the floor underneath seemed to be hollow. Uncle George removed the carpet and found a door beneath it. The door led to a room full of several coffins and a huge cupboard. They all huddled together and moved slowly towards the cupboard. They all had their Holy Crosses in their hands. The coffins started opening up and vampires started to rise from them. They held their Crosses with full courage and faith which prevented the vampires from attacking them but they were slowly progressing towards them. However Raj was attacked from behind by one of the vampires and his Holy Cross fell down from his hand. Vijay immediately started chanting the Gayatri mantra again. The vampires got burnt with immediate effect but Raj also got burnt as he had also become a vampire by that time. They all mourned for Raj's loss of life but realised that the Gayatri mantra was another tool to defend themselves from the vampire. They opened the cupboard and found the dagger in it. Uncle George dipped the dagger in the Holy water and made it ready to kill Johan Smith. They moved out of the room and waited for Johan Smith's arrival again. Uncle George told them that he would come back to his coffin at the time of dawn which was the only time he could be killed and hence the room must be made a trap for him. The room was sprinkled with the Holy water by which he would get bound. The chanting of the Gayatri mantra would start burning him and therefore he would not be able to do any harm to them. The opportunity would be utilised to stab him right through the heart with the dagger to finish him and as per plan they sprinkled the room with Holy water and hid in the room waiting for Johan Smith's arrival.

It was 4 o'clock in the morning. It was the time for dawn and Uncle George quickly informed them to stay alert because Johan Smith would fly into his coffin and hence the Holy water could not do any harm to him and moreover if he got into his coffin once then it would be impossible for them to kill him that day. They would then have to start their fight again the next night.

Soon the huge bat entered the room and the coffin opened up on its own. Vijay started chanting the Gayatri mantra again and the bat started to burn and took the shape of Johan Smith. He got bound by the Holy water but still threw Vijay down on the floor with a great might. The eyes of him were as red as blood. Uncle George warned Dennis not to look into his eyes as he would get hypnotised but the warning was late. Dennis was already hypnotised and Uncle George immediately grabbed the dagger out of Dennis' hand and thrust into the vampire Johan Smith's heart. He soon turned into stone. Dennis and Vijay had both lost their senses. Uncle George put Johan Smith's body into the coffin and looked upon Dennis and Vijay. Slowly they regained their consciousness and went out of the palace. The gate of the palace was again bound by the chains and the huge lock but that time they inscribed upon the walls of the palace not to open the gate under any circumstances.

The Revenge

It was one o' clock at night. Rohan was driving his new SUV car at the top gear. He always liked to drive at freaking high speed at night. He took the highway to enjoy his fast and furious ride. He switched on his car's music system and the loud music of death metal could be heard from distant places as the road was completely desolate.

He was driving at a tremendous high speed and the cool misty air was striking his face severely. All of a sudden, someone came in front of the car. The car was at such a high speed that he could not apply the brakes and ran over the person. He then applied the brakes and the tyres screeched to a halt.

He got out of the car to check who it was. He saw an old woman in tattered clothes, bleeding profusely after being hit by his car. He thought against of helping the poor old woman and left her to die on the road as no one had witnessed him running over her. He went back to his car and drove away back to his home quickly. He washed the tyres of his car himself to remove the blood stains so that he could cover up his crime properly.

He was unable to sleep the whole night. He was thinking of the old lady and the accident that had happened. He was also in fear that if police investigates properly and find him guilty, then what could be the consequences. The next morning, he switched on the news channel on TV but there was no news about the accident. He did not go to his office on that day as he was very much disturbed by that incident.

It was late evening when he again switched on the TV to check out the news channel and that time he saw about the accident. Police concluded that since the old lady was very poor, she had committed suicide and wrapped up the case. The police did not want actually to investigate into that matter and waste their time. Rohan was immensely satisfied with the news. He went downstairs in his garage to check his car. To his horror, blood was spilling from the tyres of his car. He immediately started to wash the tyres of his car. He continued to wash the tyres for two hours but to no avail. An old lady's laughter reverberated in the entire garage. Rohan was in shock and trembled with fear. He ran back to his room, closing the doors and windows and closed himself in his room to protect himself. The door of his room opened up slowly with a screeching sound. A shadow of an old bent lady entered into the room. There was no figure but a shadow. The shadow was approaching nearer to Rohan and he started screaming and throwing whatever he was getting to clutch at the shadow but to no avail. He ran out of his room and ran downstairs to save his life. The headlight of his car switched on its own. It had taken start. He could see very well that there was no one driving his car but it started to come forward towards him. He started to run at his highest pace wanting to save his life but his car was chasing him on its own.

Suddenly he saw that the car had stopped quite a few yards back. He turned back and looked at his car panting for breath after running for so long at his highest pace. He then realized that he had reached the place where the accident had occurred. He turned in front and saw the poor old lady standing straight in front of his eyes. He was spellbound and could not move an inch. The car started again and drove at a tremendous speed hitting him straight in the mid-section of his body.

The Cries

After several years of struggling, Vikas achieved a great success. He cracked the IAS examination and was very happy to get the offer of the post of Block Development Officer. He soon had to relocate to the place where his office was (the name of the place cannot be disclosed). His well decorated bungalow was on the banks of the river. It was a place of historical interest. He was a student of History and therefore enjoyed the place even more. As he was from a lower middle class family, he could not believe his fortune of enjoying the comfort of the luxurious bungalow. The bungalow had guards, well-maintained garden with full of flowers, servants and also the white Ambassador car which he had always dreamt of.

In the initial days he had to work even after the office hours to understand everything about his job as it happens with every new- comer in a company. He did go through each and every file to understand what extra work needed to be done. The first month was too hectic for him to even have lunch, dinner, etc. properly. His habit of going out for a morning walk and evening walk was also gone due to work pressure. After about six months or so when he understood all his work and responsibilities properly, he started to take care of his health again. He again started his old habit of going out for a morning and evening walk daily. He felt a lot relieved after the tedious work for about six months.

One evening when he went out for his walk, he sat down at a roadside tea-stall to have a cup of tea. He thought of his old memories when he used to have tea from the road-side tea stalls and used to read the newspaper from there. He started to chat with the shop-owner and in the meanwhile made friendship with him. He got to know that the tea shop-owner was from Bihar. His name was Devender and was running his business there for about ten years or so. Vikas also introduced himself to him and exclaimed about the beauty of that place. Devender kept silent about that remark of his. After a small pause in the conversation, Devender said that he must not roam around in the night. Vikas asked for the reason why but Devender carefully surpassed the question.

Slowly some days passed by and their friendship got even stronger. It was getting hotter and humid day by day. One night, there happened some major fault and the entire town plunged into darkness. There was load-shedding everywhere and Vikas' bungalow was also having no electricity. Feeling hot in his bungalow, Vikas decided to stroll around the nearby areas to have some relief under the open moonlit sky.

He went towards the riverside to enjoy the beauty of Mother Nature. He was sitting on the banks of the river. A fresh breeze was blowing over his face. He was enjoying the sweet sound of the ripples of the river when all of a sudden he heard someone's voice weeping very badly. He immediately looked around him but could not see anyone. The cries got louder but no one could be seen. Feeling disturbed by the cries, he got back to his bungalow. He could not sleep the whole night. He was hearing the cries and sound of weeping over and over again.

He kept everything to himself and was not his natural self for two days. He was really disturbed a lot and kept quiet. He again decided to go back to the riverside to find out if there was anything that was making the noise. He sat down by the riverside again. Two hours had passed and he fell asleep by the banks of the river as a cool breeze was blowing. It was midnight, when the sound of someone weeping badly broke his sleep. The cries got louder. He shouted, "Who is it? Why aren't you coming in front?" The cries got clearer. He could hear many people weeping and begging for mercy. He could hear the chopping off the heads of many people. It was the sound of mass killing when suddenly everything stopped. Vikas fainted after that incident.

He regained consciousness the next morning. He did not go back to his bungalow but went straight to his friend Devender's tea-stall. He explained everything that he had experienced the other night. Devender kept silent for a while after listening to all what he had heard from Vikas. He then said that he had warned him previously not to roam about at night. Vikas was now desperate to know the reason why.

Devender then said that it was indeed a place of historical interest as there were many monuments and other areas of historical interest but there remained many bad incidents in history which continues to haunt even today. People visit and enjoy the scenic beauty of the beautiful monument but it is said that the monument is also haunted. On no moon and full moon nights, many people have heard the cries, the sound of Hindustani Classical music and the sound of ankle bells. The sound of weeping and cries of people asking for mercy is heard every night by the banks of the river. It remains in history that the architects and all the people who had worked to build the monument were beheaded. Even their families were wiped off because the emperor thought that their descendants might have inborn talents to design a similar monument which he never wanted.

The cries were that of the people who had worked for the monument and their families. Vikas applied for his transfer that very day as the memories kept on haunting him. The sound of the people crying and weeping can still be heard even today.

Fact of Life

After several years of brainstorming I have come to a conclusion about life. I always hunted for answers of many questions that aroused in my mind about life.

The questions are as follows:

How does life come in the pre-stage of birth?

What controls life? Human beings, plants, animals, etc. are all systems like an engine but unlike engines, these have life.

What does happen after death? Why does a person die?

The conclusion that I have come upon is that electricity is the source of life. Let us take the example of a human being. Human beings have electricity in their body. Body is mainly an engine. It needs food to work properly by the means of energy. Thus the electricity supply in the body is maintained. Epilepsy is one kind of illness which gives the example of electric charges in our body. If sudden electric bursts occur in brain which is not normal, the person becomes unconscious and seizures occur, this is known as epilepsy. When the flow of electricity in our body becomes weak on ageing, death comes closer. The cells in our body die slowly and electric power in the body goes down. Finally when the power ceases, death occurs. Now the ultimate life that is present in every living cell comprises of oxygen, hydrogen, nitrogen, carbon dioxide in a particular proportion that is bound by the electric power. When the electric power becomes loose, these components get out of the body and diffuse in air.

As it diffuses in air, the electric power that binds the components decreases and the lighter it gets, the quicker it moves upwards. It crosses the different spheres of the atmosphere over a period of time. When it reaches the ionosphere, the components again get charged and become heavy to reach the earth. It enters into an embryo and thus gives life back to a new organism in whatever form it might be. This cycle continues and this is how re-birth also occurs.

This is however my sole assumption about the fact of life as how it occurs, how it is controlled and how re-birth occurs which may be true or may not be. This is truly a matter of debate. As from my assumption, I also believe that life exists everywhere and it is of two forms. One is static and the other is dynamic. The dynamic life is that we all know about that is the life which exists in plants, animals, human beings, etc. but the static life is the life that exists in the so called non-living things on earth.

Everything on earth can be broken down to the ultimate ions as protons, electrons and neutrons which mean that everything consists of the basic source of life that is electricity. All things on the earth either conduct electricity or they do not which can be determined by the presence of free electrons in them. Hence from my assumption, I conclude that the so called non-living things have life in the static form.

In fact many people study paranormal science and they have found unnatural existence. They use electro-magnetic devices to detect the existence of spirits. There are also many places in the world that are declared as haunted. In India also, the ASI (Archaeological Survey of India) has declared many places as haunted and put up the sign board displaying "Staying here after sunset is strictly prohibited" like in Bhangarh.